Licensed exclusively to Top That Publishing Ltd
Tide Mill Way, Woodbridge, Suffolk, IP12 1AP, UK
www.topthatpublishing.com
Copyright © 2014 Tide Mill Media
All rights reserved
0 2 4 6 8 9 7 5 3 1
Printed and bound in China

ISBN 978-1-78445-127-1

A catalogue record for this book is available from the British Library

Old MacDonald had a barn, E-I-E-I-O!
And in his barn lived all his friends, E-I-E-I-O!

Two owls, some ducks, a dog and cat. Even snakes! How about that?
Old MacDonald had a barn, E-I-E-I-O!

**With a barn like this and all those friends, there's lots of work to do.
But Old MacDonald didn't mind. He'd work the whole day through!**

He milked his cows, then fed them grain, then he'd do it all again!
Old MacDonald had a barn, E-I-E-I-O!

**All the barn loved dear Old Mac,
And thought they'd let him know.**

They made a plan all by themselves, E-I-E-I-O!

While Old MacDonald slept that night, his friends made quite a show.

They fixed that barn up just like new, E-I-E-I-O!

Next morning when the sun came up, Cock-a-Doodle-Doo!
Old MacDonald went outside, he had some chores to do.

The animals made quite a plan, with nothing left to chance,

When the barn doors opened up that day,
They had a Big Barn Dance!

Yes, Old MacDonald had a barn, E-I-E-I-O!
And in this barn they had a dance, E-I-E-I-O!

Old MacDonald had a barn, E-I-E-I-O!
And in his barn lived all his friends, E-I-E-I-O!

Two owls, some ducks, a dog and cat. Even snakes! How about that?
Old MacDonald had a barn, E-I-E-I-O!

With a barn like this and all those friends, there's lots of work to do.
But Old MacDonald didn't mind. He'd work the whole day through!

He milked his cows, then fed them grain, then he'd do it all again!
Old MacDonald had a barn, E-I-E-I-O!

All the barn loved dear Old Mac,
And thought they'd let him know.
They made a plan all by themselves, E-I-E-I-O!

While Old MacDonald slept that night,
his friends made quite a show.
They fixed that barn up just like new, E-I-E-I-O!

Next morning when the sun came up, Cock-a-Doodle-Doo!
Old MacDonald went outside, he had some chores to do.

The animals made quite a plan, with nothing left to chance,
When the barn doors opened up that day,
They had a Big Barn Dance!

Yes, Old MacDonald had a barn, E-I-E-I-O!
And in this barn they had a dance, E-I-E-I-O!

CK-A-
ODLE-
DOO!

THE END

LOOK OUT!

If you liked Old MacDonald's Barn try these other great titles:

Santa's Toy Shop
ISBN 978-1-78445-129-5

Jolly Roger's Pirate Ship
ISBN 978-1-78445-128-8